PUPPY TAKEOVER

PUPPIES TAKEOVER SCHOOL

BY EASTON LOWE

With Special Thanks to my DADDY

Message from the Author,

Hello everyone! I am so excited that you are reading my book that I wrote with my daddy. I am so happy how this has turned out and I really hope you enjoy it as much as I do.

I love puppies and reading books about them. I have a big fluffy black and brown puppy with white marks on him. He loves to play, go on walks, and use up all his energy and then take a nap. He even enjoys going for rides with me and my mom in the car and hanging his head out the window.

This book is the greatest thing I have ever created and am so happy that other kids are getting a chance to enjoy it.

Please feel free to let all your friends and family know about it. I hope lots and lots of kids around the world read this book and get to enjoy the puppy adventures.

Please also take time and leave a comment about the book or a message on Amazon for me to read. I hope to hear from all of you that got the book and that you really liked it.

If all goes well, I am going to write another book and even hope to write more in the future.

Thank you again for reading my book. I wish all of you the very best!

Easton Lowe

TABLE OF CONTENTS

CHAPTER 1 – SNORING POLICE

It was a peaceful and sunny day for the officers at the local police station, who didn't have a care in the world. The station was quiet, and the police officers had dozed off into a deep sleep. They were even snoring and enjoying their dreams…

Suddenly, the loud ring of the phone startled Officer Jeff and caused him to flip out of his chair!

"Wooooaaaa!" He answered the phone and mumbled to whomever was on the phone with him. "What the what!"

Hearing that, the other officers gathered around Jeff.

He continued, "What! Ran off?"

"What is it, Jeff?" An officer said, but Officer Jeff didn't answer.

"Puppies!" He suddenly exclaimed and the officers gasped.

Officer Jeff put down the phone and said, "There are puppies on the loose. They were last seen running towards the elementary school. We have to get them."

CHAPTER 2 – OFF TO PUPPY PARADISE

The officers ran down the hallway of the police station and out the front door, stumbling into their cars with incredible speed. They drove off and raced to the school as quick as they could to help find the puppies. But maybe they were *too* excited because they came in too fast and smashed into a set of trash cans! The officers jumped out of their cars and ran into the school. They looked around and to their super surprise, all they could see were puppies, *puppies everywhere*! It was a puppy paradise!

One cute, little, fluffy puppy jumped up and opened the front door to the school. Five little husky puppies pushed each of the officers out of the school. Police Officer Jeff was speechless.

CHAPTER 3 – CRAZY RED ROOM TAKEOVER

The police marched back into the school and dashed into the Red Room. They saw a puppy chewing on a baseball, but before they could do anything, he got the entire ball into his mouth and started slobbering all over it. They saw another puppy, a labradoodle, bouncing on a teacher's desk. Then one more, chunky puppy, chewing up pictures that he had knocked down from the walls. The other one they saw was all the way up on a ladder and writing on the chalk board. The officers looked at each other and laughed out loud because the little brown doggie wrote, "Puppy's Rule"!

CHAPTER 4 – PUPPIES TAKEOVER SPECIALS

Each officer went through the school to check on different areas and rooms. One officer went into the art room and saw puppies drawing pictures of themselves and leaving heart-prints with their paws on canvases. Another officer checked the music room and heard puppies barking Twinkle Twinkle Little Star with a golden retriever directing them by waving his paws up in the air. One was playing the piano, another one was playing the saxophone, two were playing the guitar, and the last two were playing the drums.

CHAPTER 4 – PUPPIES TAKEOVER SPECIALS - CONTINUED

Another officer hurried to the gym and to his amazement, he saw puppies doing all kinds of exercises. Some were doing pushups, some were doing sit-ups, but what amazed the officer the most was one strong puppy doing chin-ups. There was a big, spotted Dalmatian that was coaching all the puppies in the gym too.

The final policeman ran down to the tech lab room and to his disbelief, he saw puppies playing video games! A few were working on creating a new tablet game called Puppy Obstacle Course. Some even had headsets with microphones on them and barked away to each other. Of course, the officers couldn't understand their "woofs."

CHAPTER 5 – PUPPIES HERE, PUPPIES THERE, PUPPIES EVERYWHERE

The police officers regrouped back at the entrance. They decided to look through each classroom, starting with the kindergarten rooms. The first room was full of puppies learning to count. The puppy trying to teach didn't know how to count either, so this was obviously very funny to see. The officers moved on to the 1st grade classroom and they saw puppies sitting around a bigger doggie telling a story and learning how to read. Next came the 2nd grade classrooms and they found puppies learning how to write paragraphs and making up funny stories. After that, the officers went off to the 3rd grade classroom and saw puppies learning about history with a puppy-teacher dressed up in an old-time costume. The officers made their way down to the 4th grade classroom and even though they thought what they saw at specials was weird and amazing, nothing could have prepared them for this sight. They saw puppies taking tests for the Extended Learning program in meteorology and astronomy. Not quite sure if they got the answers right or not, but they sure were enjoying themselves. One puppy was leaping up into the air trying to grab a fake star hung from the ceiling. The officers started laughing and even snorted a little bit causing all the puppies to turn and stare at them.

CHAPTER 6 – SCHOOL BUS TAKEOVER

After searching around the school some more, the officers started noticing less and less puppies around and were wondering where they had run off to. They noticed two little puppies following them around. The two puppies ran around them and headed towards the exit of the school. Officer Jeff was wondering where all these little puppies were heading off to, so they all followed them out the exit.

"Oh, boy!" Officer Jeff exclaimed as he saw all the puppies piled into a few school buses! They noticed big dogs had joined the puppy takeover and in each school bus, a big dog was in the driver seat. When all the puppies got on the buses and in their seats, they shut the doors, honked the bus horn and off they went out of the school parking lot. Officer Jeff told all the other policemen to get in their cars and follow them. As they drove down the road, the school buses were swerving all over and even tipping up on two wheels! More police officers joined in on the chase. In disbelief, people pulled off the roads when they saw puppies and dogs driving school buses. Still, onward the puppies went.

CHAPTER 7 – AMUSEMENT PARK TAKEOVER

The puppies drove and drove, and the officers weren't sure where they were heading until they saw signs for an amusement park ahead. They knew just where the puppies were heading.

Once they arrived, the puppies parked the buses and jumped out. They ran up to the entrance and gathered around like they were making a plan. At that point, they all started to run into the amusement park in multiple directions. The officers made their own game plan and split up to follow them all over the park. The first group of puppies were riding on roller coasters like Thunderback, The Mountaineer, Space Jumper and the Wild Wild Racers. The next group took over the snack bars, enjoying all the delicious foods and treats. They each ate lots of snacks like popcorn, pretzels, hotdogs and cotton candy and got their tummies all full. But later, they all started feeling a little queasy when trying to ride the rides again. Maybe they shouldn't have eaten so much food and so many treats all at once. Ugh!

CHAPTER 7 – AMUSEMENT PARK TAKEOVER - CONTINUED

In another area of the amusement park, a group of puppies took over the awesome amusement park dog show. They did lots of tricks and received a standing ovation from all the people there. One of the tricks—a puppy named Fluffy—performed was running around on a giant ball. Others named Henry and Jack jumped through giant hoops. Another puppy named Carter stood on a pop bottle, on top of a baseball bat, balanced on a barrel, sitting on a large ball, on top of a small box! Say what!

"Amazing," the crowd yelled, "utterly amazing!"

That was the grand finale of the dog show. All the dogs had had their fun at the amusement park and headed back to the school buses with the officers following close behind. But every time the officers were close enough to catch them, they lost their concentration because of the amazing things the puppies were doing and forgot to wrangle the puppies up.

CHAPTER 8 – CRAZY BUS RIDE BACK TO SCHOOL

Inside the busses, the puppies drew comic books. One puppy named Gracie wrote the stories and another named Andy illustrated the comics by drawing crazy pictures all over the paper. As they were creating the comics, the other puppies were acting out the stories, pretending to fly, leaping over buildings and being superheroes.

The police officers were right behind them with lights and sirens blasting. They were yelling with megaphones telling them to "Pull over! Pull over! Please pull over the bus!"

The puppies got excited and some even climbed on top of the buses and started acting like they were surfing. They were howling and barking and having a crazy good time. Luckily, with all that craziness going on, they still made it back to the school safely. All the puppies and dogs ran off the buses and back into the elementary school.

CHAPTER 9 – TIME TO GO HOME, PUPPIES

Officer Jeff carefully led all the other police officers through the open school yards and back into the school to round up all the puppies and dogs, once and for all. The puppies were finally starting to slow down a little bit, but the officers were still barely keeping up with them. Officer Jeff said, "boy oh boy, these cute little puppies sure do have a lot of energy." His other officers started laughing and agreeing with him and said, "just like a lot of little kids we know!" Then suddenly, the puppies and dogs started barking and barking and barking as if they were laughing and agreeing with the police officers!

CHAPTER 9 – TIME TO GO HOME, PUPPIES - CONTINUED

Once inside, the officers saw the husky puppies that had earlier pushed them out of the school. The husky puppies were super exhausted and instead of pushing the officers out of the school, they came up and started giving them puppy hugs and puppy kisses. The other puppies were also really tired from all of the excitement and crazy fun they had all day. They joined the huskies and started giving puppy hugs and kisses to all the police officers. Officer Jeff told all the other cops to each take a group of puppies to their cars and go locate their home neighborhoods to get them back to their owners. The puppies cooperated with the officers this time and went with them peacefully and quietly.

Each of the police officers drove off in different directions and headed to the puppies' homes. Once there, they let each puppy out and the puppies ran up to their owners and jumped into their arms with great excitement to be back home. They licked all over their families' faces and barked with joy!

1 YEAR LATER……

It is a beautiful and sunny day with not a care in the world to be had. All the police officers are relaxing at their police station. Officer Jeff is taking a nap at his desk with his feet up when all of a sudden, the phone rings and startles him right out of his chair.

"Whooooaaaa!"

There is a loud voice on the other end yelling something about puppies and the new, huge FIRE STATION!

"What the whhaaaaa…"

The End….Until next time!

Made in the USA
Middletown, DE
22 September 2020